Poetic Remedies for Troubled Times from

ASK BABA YAGA

Other books by Taisia Kitaiskaia

Ask Baba Yaga: Otherworldly Advice for Everyday Troubles

Literary Witches: A Celebration of Magical Women Writers

The Nightgown and Other Poems

Poetic Remedies for Troubled Times from

ASK BABA YAGA

Taisia Kitaiskaia

Illustrations by Katy Horan

Andrews McMeel
PUBLISHING®

Andrews McMeel Publishing
a division of Andrews McMeel Universal
1130 Walnut Street, Kansas City, Missouri 64106

www.andrewsmcmeel.com

20 21 22 23 24 SDB 10 9 8 7 6 5 4 3 2 1

ISBN: 978-1-5248-5503-1

Library of Congress Control Number: 2020930963

Editor: Allison Adler
Art Director: Holly Swayne
Illustrations: Katy Horan
Production Editor: Amy Strassner
Production Manager: Cliff Koehler

ATTENTION: SCHOOLS AND BUSINESSES
Andrews McMeel books are available at quantity discounts
with bulk purchase for educational, business, or sales
promotional use. For information, please e-mail the
Andrews McMeel Publishing Special Sales Department:
specialsales@amuniversal.com.

CONTENTS

GOOD IN YR BONES . . . 41

THE FOREST PATH . . . 67

PREFACE

I wrote this second volume of advice from Baba Yaga because I needed the crone more than ever, and I felt others might need her, too.

Who is Baba Yaga? You can read her own thoughts on the subject ("Who are you?" on page xii), but we can begin with the facts. Baba Yaga is a prominent figure in Slavic folklore, an old witch haunting the fairy tales and woods of Eastern Europe for centuries, if not longer (like her ambiguous character, Baba's origins are difficult to pin down). She lives in a magic hut, which has big, thick chicken legs and a mind of its own. A fence of bones and skulls guards the house. When she's not hanging out in her hut, Baba Yaga goes on mysterious adventures in the forest, using a large mortar and pestle to get around. If her mortar drags on the forest floor, she's quick to cover her tracks with a birch broom. From time to time, humans come to Baba Yaga's hut--seeking shelter, a special object or person, advice. They find her when they've been cast out and abandoned, when all is lost. At this juncture, Baba Yaga can be villainous and hungry, even trying to push the person into her oven for a snack. Or she can be tricksy and demanding, putting the poor soul to work. Or she can be a guardian, giving over all the answers and an enchanted object to boot.

Often, she's all of these things in one tale, which
is part of what I love about her: no one knows
what she'll do next. Born in eastern Russia, I
spent the first five years of my life in the woods
of Lake Baikal, and Baba Yaga lived there, too.
I felt her among the mushrooms and berries and
animals; I imagined her sitting in the dark of her
hut, knitting something wily and strange. Around
her head, she wore a kerchief, like any Russian
grandmother, and she did feel like a grandmother
to me--formidable and unpredictable, sure, but
ultimately nurturing and wise. I trusted her to know
all that there was to know. I admired her wild life
in the woods. I wanted her near me always, setting
an example, looking out.

During 2013-2015, I wrote an advice column in Baba
Yaga's voice for a site called the Hairpin, later
collecting the pieces in my book *Ask Baba Yaga:
Otherworldly Advice for Everyday Troubles*. The
pieces featured real questions from real strangers
on love, belonging, and purpose, along with Baba
Yaga's answers, written in a poetic style all her
own. When the book came out in 2017, the world felt
more disorienting than ever, and I knew I wasn't
done talking to Baba Yaga. Now *I* was the one who
needed Baba to make sense of things. What would
she say about climate change, global disasters, the
failure of our leaders and neighbors, identity,
and oppressive systems? When I put out a call for
more questions for Baba Yaga, worries about what

will happen to us in these troubled times surfaced alongside the everyday worries.

While Baba Yaga can't replace a therapist or a friend, she offers a different kind of perspective-- an ancient outsider to our human affairs, a forest witch who speaks in the language of trees and ponds and fairy tales, an immortal witness to our folly and suffering. I was raised to give my unsolvable problems over to something larger than myself, and for me, that larger presence is Baba Yaga. I hope that you, too, can find some refuge in Baba's words.

Taisia Kitaiskaia

WHO ARE YOU?

Dear Baba Yaga,

Who are you?

BABA YAGA:

I am the unknown soul, the chaos in the mud. The
snake roiling in butter, the nightmare in the bark,
the owl sleeping on the nightmare.; In each egg I
am the cracking and the bird, the delirious chicken
scratching yr wound. You reach your hand into my
dress, come up with diamonds,then worms. Ha!: I'm
your fear turned inside out like a sleeve. Try and
catch me by the tail, I'll coil up in yr goblet.) I
am yr grandmother, the pelt on the wall that wanders
off. I'm the warm earth you'll be buried in, the
wind washing yr living hair. I did not come here for
you, but I will stay and watch. : When World first
exploded, I oozed out. I will survive the next great
shattering--I am the shattering.

LOVE CAULDRONS

Dear Baba Yaga,

I'm a thirty-eight-year-old woman who wants to date men, but I've always been terrified of them and have never been in a relationship. My fear has only grown with #MeToo, and sometimes I feel it's truly impossible to find a good-hearted male feminist--someone who would see me as an equal, pure and simple. I've already kind of given up and have found happiness in my work and social life. Is this single-for-life existence the future for women?

BABA YAGA:

All my living I have been an old woman, in the woods ;alone. I do what I like : I muddy & sweep my hut, carry myself into the sky & listen to what it says, I gather mushrooms, terrorize foxes & men with my fiendly claws & gait, laugh a long time into a bucket until it laughs back with a spit, breathe as a stone at the bottom of a creek--& many other things I do not say. But none of it is done from fearing. Poke at the fear as into the dying fire in yr hearth: which way do the sparks go, how does the fire hiss? If you , choose my life--know you are choosing it, not hiding in the woods.

HOW DO I FALL IN LOVE?

Dear Baba Yaga,

I am in my thirties, and I've never had a
relationship. I've used my independence as a way
to justify my lack of partners to others, but I
actually feel an overwhelming desire to experience
romantic love. My biggest fear is that I may not
be able to be really intimate with anyone. I'm
afraid that I will never find the love I am looking
for, and ashamed to admit my inexperience even if
I should find someone, and--though I hate to admit
it--I am lonely. I guess my question is--how do you
fall in love?

BABA YAGA:

To fall in love is to encounter yrself in the full
sun , and you are afraid of the strange things
you've burrowed away.-- But to fall in love, you
must bite into the apple of yr shame ; you must hold
yr small body in your arms and know yrself to be
large. (It is like those times when you see your
Self peeking, frightened, from behind a door. ; This
time, open the door & walk out. That's all..

WHAT MAKES A CONNECTION SPECIAL?

Dear Baba Yaga,

Why do certain people spark things within you
that others can't? Are special connections truly
possible? How can you tell when it's happened,
Baba Yaga?

BABA YAGA:

Each human's love is kept in a secret egg. For some,
the egg hides in a duck's belly, and the duck's
inside a rabbit, the rabbit in a chest, chest in
an oak, oak on a far island. --For others, the
egg is balanced on top of their head, where anyone
can reach it. ; Not everyone knows where to find
another's egg, not everyone is interested. Humans
are riddle-solvers & animals both. A lover must
solve the egg riddle with the mind & eat the egg
with the body. , You'll know,when you hear the click
of teeth .

WHAT IF I FALL FOR MY COWORKER?

Dear Baba Yaga,

I've been slowly falling for my coworker. We have
been working together for two years, and every day
that I see him, my appreciation and attraction grow
stronger. I don't want him to know, and I don't want
to make things weird at work. What can a gal do in
this sort of mess?

BABA YAGA:

You are two frogs on one small lily pad : of course
his beauty calls to you, along with his croak, if
he be a comely or goodly frog at all. It is likely
he sees yr beauty also. ,But what now? There are 3
ways: You can sit on the lily pad in quiet, yr heart
a glowing bead - you can speak & stick yr frog-
tongues together - you can wait until one frog hops
to another lily pad, & watch what happens with the
call. You are a free frog after all ,.

WHAT CAN I DO ABOUT A LIBIDO MISMATCH?

Dear Baba Yaga,

I'm a newlywed who, after years of working through PTSD, has finally been able to access my sexuality. But now I find that my libido is higher than my husband's. How do I accept the difference in our sex drives without feeling rejected and lonely?

BABA YAGA:

When you were lost in the thistle, wasn't yr body inescapably itself, and nothing could change the movements of yr blood? Now that you walk in the clearing, full of sun, you want yr husband to join you . But he is in some other woods. All bodies are innocent & cannot help how they feel.Be generous, like the clearing : be large with yr husband, as you wanted someone to be large with Thistle-you . Seek yr pleasure , but without demands.

Dear Baba Yaga,

My spouse and I are not as compatible as we once
thought. We love each other, but we have such
different wants, needs, and ambitions. I am torn
between working on the relationship and following
my fire. How do I make this decision?

BABA YAGA:

This choice is an angry chicken in yr arms:
Scratching, pecking, writhing . You can barely)
think , so Noisy is this chicken, so sore are yr
limbs. ;Set the chicken down, watch her run up the
road all a-clucking. -- Stand still , breathing
with yr bones & blood. , Unburdened, now what do
you want?

Dear Baba Yaga,

My husband recently expressed an interest in opening
our relationship to other partners. I've told him
that this makes me uncomfortable, but I worry that
I'm keeping him from fully enjoying his life. What
should I do?

BABA YAGA:

Yr husband sees a river with floating candles & the
laughter of maidens in the reeds. You see ravens
carrying the bones of yr marriage. : Do not walk
into what spells doom for you. , If the river voices
call loud to yr husband, he may choose to wade into
the water, and the thread between you will snap.
-- But perhaps you have already been dwelling far
apart, the thread so tense with distance? .

HOW DO I GET OVER A CRUEL REJECTION?

Dear Baba Yaga,

I gave someone my whole heart; we were making plans
to get married. In the end, they rejected me because
of my appearance. This has destroyed me, leaving me
feeling ashamed and unworthy. Time has passed, but
I still haven't recovered. How do I let this go and
trust that I am worthy of love?

BABA YAGA:

The rat you speak of was cruel,confused. . Are you
not a garden? Does not yr mind have many hills and
lakes and swans? , Are you not made of the same fine
linen as rabbits & temples? , Did you not carry love
like holy water in yr palms & let the rat drink?
; In the mirror, I say to myself: Any-one should
cherish to see this ugly face. & no-one is as ugly
as the Baba, ha! See, you were not cherished as you
should be . : Cast this happening , like a snotty
handkerchief , back to whom it belongs, and be with
yrself as you truly are . This is not yr shame, but
the rat's; & the rat should live with it, not you.

Dear Baba Yaga,

My fiancé left me a couple months ago, his reasons
being that we were holding each other back in our
desires and goals. I miss him and love him deeply,
and I know he loves me. I don't know how to let go
and move on without retaining hope of being with him
again someday.

BABA YAGA:

; You hold the rope to a boat taken suddenly by sea.
. Hold it as long as you like,in one hand. & use
the other hand to feed yrself , drink from goblets,
and wave to birds who may guide you. Soon., you will
tire of the old rope, so scratchy & bringing you
nothing. Soon , you must grasp yr life with both
hands.) But for now, keep whatever comforts you --
no one can grudge you a simple rope.

WHAT IF I NEVER FIND LOVE AGAIN?

Dear Baba Yaga,

How do I deal with the fear that I'll never find
love again? I'm getting older, I have health
problems, and I feel like I'm losing my spark. I
want to love and be loved, but I'm worried I'll
spend the remainder of my days alone.

BABA YAGA:

Yr body is a wish in the river, weeds round yr
wrists , Moon bringing you a tincture. At the bottom
of the river, ghosts toss stones to one another &
light candles in their bellies.) You do not need
to wrap yrself around a spark , you need only to lie
open, your back in the dark water. & Every-thing
has its fear--the leaves & stumps, the nails in the
wood, the eye of the fish. :You are never alone in
the mystery : you can Be love itself , a candle in
the belly of the ghost.

Dear Baba Yaga,

I feel like my parents don't deserve to be at my upcoming wedding. My father was abusive during my childhood, my alcoholic mother denies the abuse, and neither has made any effort to meet my supportive, lovely partner. But if I don't invite them, other family members will ask questions. What do I do?

BABA YAGA:

Is yr wedding for pleasing guests, or for adorning yrself with wild fruits & riding a creature into the banquet? -- If some of both, dream up what would make the twisted ones tolerable . If nothing would make them so, bar their entry, hold yr Golden staff & decree to yr guests the how and why of yr occasion. , If puzzlement lingers, so be it: When you are apple-crowned & riding a pig with the lovely one, who cares about a few question marks?

WHAT DO I DO ABOUT MY PARTNER'S TOUCHY FATHER?

Dear Baba Yaga,

My partner's dad, while not a lecherous man, is overly touchy: hand on my shoulder or small of my back, unwanted hugs and kisses on the forehead. It makes me feel powerless, embarrassed, and then angry for allowing a man to make me feel this way. I don't know how to bring this up to my partner. What do I do? (P.S. If I felt I was in any danger, I would seek serious help.)

BABA YAGA:

Humans are always slithering their snake tongues on each other, little slug trails, reaching & licking . It is hateful , Baba would chop off their tails! But for you, it is trickier : You want to make everyone so happy, but your happiness is the only kind you can hold. . Bring yr discomforts and angers to the one you love, tell them what you have told me. Either they, after quieting a belly of odd feelings, will take care & do what is right--or the whole family is rotten.

Dear Baba Yaga,

I'm bisexual, and my partner is straight. There has
always been some tension between me and a few of his
family members, and I just found out that some of
the tension is due to my sexuality. How do I remain
connected with the family while staying true to
who I am?

BABA YAGA:

These tense ones are children hiding behind
toadstools , afraid even of the crows flying dark
in genius. How sorry,they have touched so few of
Earth's glories. : So walk tall , since the woods
belong to you , and pat the heads of the small ones,
who one day may see--& if they holler and tantrum,
send them to their rooms.

Dear Baba Yaga,

How do I connect with people on a daily basis in
this ever-changing world? How do I know when it's
safe to engage with people I don't know? I'm well
adapted to city life, where ignoring others is an
ingrained behavior.

BABA YAGA:

All you mammals want, seals or bears or humans, is
to squish yr bodies together, rub snouts in fur, be
close to another's warmth. . No mortal is different
from you, very few want to hurt you. (How to tame
a wild bear? Put out crumbs, lump of meat, rip of
bread, with yr own living hand, until the bear
comes closer. Every day, call out the beasts with
little morsels : bring them the same things you
like, nuts & jokes. Many cakes later, you may be
less feral yrself.

Dear Baba Yaga,

I'm not great at meeting new people. It can take a
lot of emotional energy to make myself get dressed
and out of the house to see people I already know
and like, so the stress of meeting new people can
and has literally kept me up at night. How do I
put myself out there and enjoy others without
draining myself?

BABA YAGA:

Alone You and Village You stand apart , shy &
fearful. Measure their distance with a thread: a
long thread is misery. ; Now . tie the thread to
Alone You's wrist, put the other end in Village
You's hand. , Take the two selves on a walk. When
the thread tightens, slacken the hold,beckon
Village You closer to the other. -- Practice this
strolling,. Soon the two will be dancing slow &
sweaty together, the dreaded thread trampled under
all your feets.

Dear Baba Yaga,

So many of my friends have abusive ex-partners. What
is the best way to go about cursing said abusers?

BABA YAGA:

Such people are cursed already. ;Hold up, instead,
a skull-lantern from my fence, and say to them
this spell:

> *Stare into these glowing eyes*
> *Till you are as bare in yr knowing*
> *As this skull in its bone.*

HOW SHOULD I TREAT MY CHILDHOOD BULLIES?

Dear Baba Yaga,

I have recently become a fairly in-demand tattoo
artist, and several of my past bullies have inquired
about getting tattoos from me. Should I turn them
down for the way they've treated me, or should I
work with them and take their money anyway? Should
I settle for the vindication of knowing they enjoy
but can never have my work, or should I give them a
permanent piece of me?

BABA YAGA:

Inked by old pain, your skin (not theirs) is of
first concern. Past as it may be, the pain comes
back with a prick: stay with the needle. Where does
the feeling live now? : Which shapes & images has
it inscribed upon yr body? Is it permanent, or does
it wash off in the bath? Before you act, look deep
inside with your inky eye.

MY FRIENDS KEEP COPYING ME--WHAT DO I DO?

Dear Baba Yaga,

My friends have a tendency to copy everything I do:
style, hobbies, ideas. Anything I feel proud of is
snatched and imitated. I feel angry and sad, like
a little kid who never gets to keep anything for
herself. How do I make these feelings pass?

BABA YAGA:

You are the first dandelion opening her petals
in the morning , then the other flowers follow. ;
Were the other dandelions never to greet the sun?
Isn't there plenty of sun for you , even with the
others looking? -- Even so, do not shoo the child
in her pouting, but give her a wink. Each flower
wants to be admired in her particularity. , Only
know, nothing has been snatched from you : you
have everything you did before, and the sun has
always shone.

WHERE IS THE LINE BETWEEN ENABLING AND SUPPORTING?

Dear Baba Yaga,

I have a friend whom I love dearly and who has had
to deal with a lot. She struggles with depression
and regularly tries therapy and medication but
always quits, which sends her into an even worse
shame spiral. I feel like my role is to be a
supportive, nonjudgmental presence, but it's hard
to see her repeatedly fall into the same patterns. I
think there may also be some addiction issues. Where
do I draw the line between supporting and enabling?

BABA YAGA:

There are many ways to harm a thrashing Goat :
Clapping or giving sweetmeats when the goat thrashes
, widening her thrashing-field so she can thrash
all the day, & so on. Standing still next to the
goat, like a lovely tree, reminds the goat of all
the world's treasures and does no harm. ; But watch:
perhaps you are tired of being a tree, or standing
so still when you have thrashings of yr own. Is yr
bark sometimes splintering with little hates towards
yr goat-friend? . Tend to yrself between goat
vigils, return to tree-shape only when yr bark is
smooth & satisfied.

AM I DOOMED TO BE A FREE THERAPIST TO MY FRIENDS?

Dear Baba Yaga,

Am I doomed to always be a free therapist to
friends? I feel like people care about me only for
the care I provide to them, not for who I genuinely
am. I am tired and scared and sad to feel unloved
except for my utility.

BABA YAGA:

Your friends are unwise, but You, too, have played
a part: why do you sit so long & listen? Over the
yearlies, you have woven others' tales into yr
braid, you have plaited yr being with listening. .
Who are you, then, without this strange,cold ribbon
in your hair?

HOW CAN I BECOME A BETTER LISTENER?

Dear Baba Yaga,

My husband told me that I don't really listen to
him, that my attention drifts when he talks to me,
and that this makes him feel lonely. I love him so
much and hate that I could treat him so poorly.
Am I a horrible, self-centered person? How can I
be better?

BABA YAGA:

Humans were molded from little rat things, surviving
among sticks. ; Of course you are small, worried,
never being where you are, listening for scary
sounds elsewhere in the forest. You are wanting to
be safe, but look here : you will never be safe,
death watches you now as yr tail switches and yr
nose sniffs the dark air. Again & again you are
afraid. So pet your rat-heart : you cannot change
its shape or tremble. But you can be still and
listen for what trances you, asking: what noise is
this? . The true music is coming from yr burrow.

Dear Baba Yaga,

One of my friends has a longtime professional
career, an expensively decorated home, and a
bourgeois lifestyle. I've had a string of lesser-
paying jobs, a house that will probably always
feel like a compromise, and a more unconventional
approach to life. Whenever she reaches out, the
prospect of seeing her fills me with anxiety. I'm
worried she will judge or misunderstand me. How do
I put aside my fear and focus on reconnecting?

BABA YAGA:

-- Your friend, she wants to be near! Perhaps she
is lonely, or feels her life is strange to you, and
is ashamed in some way you cannot imagine. Imagine
is what you must do: use yr brain to smolder up
the Invisible. Imagine what is restless & afraid &
wanting in her being, so like you. She is more than
her way of living. Doesn't your heart also want to
be near? . Let this soft creature lead the way.

HOW DO I STAY FRIENDS WITH PEOPLE WHO HAVE KIDS?

Dear Baba Yaga,

All my friends are having kids, but more and more
I think I want to stay child-free. How do I navigate
friendship with people whose lives are moving in
such a different direction?

BABA YAGA:

The trouble is when each swaddles in garments: The
Stately Garments of Her Family - or - The Luxurious
Garments of Her Freedom, and then no-one is small
and tender with each other, or spilling wine across
the table, or mixing their pains & wants into the
spill with an ungloved finger. . Drink together &
speak ! Be frank & joyous & sad with each other ,
and if you must be clothed,then wrap yr shawl
around the other's shoulders, and huddle under
it togetherly.

HOW DO I HELP MY WAYWARD TEENAGER?

Dear Baba Yaga,

My teenage daughter keeps making bad choices, and I'm afraid I'm going to lose her. Should I stop trying to help her and let her fall into the dark consequences of her actions?

BABA YAGA:

You think this daughter is a teacup you cannot drop, but she is alive and limber as a wolf: You cannot hold her or determine her fall. ; When your daughter runs from your arms, open them to Grief, the wolf you've kept pacing in yr yard. Hold Grief close, love&know her, as your daughter wanders the world & does what she will do.

HOW CAN I BE BOTH SEX POSITIVE AND
CAUTIONARY IN MY PARENTING?

Dear Baba Yaga,

While I am grateful to have had many sexual
experiences, some were rather negative and even
violent. I now have a young daughter, and I want her
to feel comfortable with and own her sexuality. But
I also want her to be aware of the dangers that can
easily befall women. How can I be both sex positive
and cautionary in my parenting?

BABA YAGA:

Do not speak to yr child in riddles, or smear
shadows round the house. ; Give yr stories to her as
stones, dark and gold, so she can know their weight
& texture for herself.) Fill her pockets with
hearty bread for every journey , & show her how to
bake it; Teach her to whistle for the wind when she
is lost,to make a nest in any lonely place ,. And do
these things for yrself , as she watches you close
-- & if there is fear in you , untouched, ferret
it out & speak to it: What yr daughter feels most,
along with yr love, are the lurking things.,

HOW CAN I BE A BETTER MOTHER?

Dear Baba Yaga,

I love my young children fiercely, but I find myself
increasingly stressed out and snappy. I'm not the
calm and unruffled mother I want to be. How do I
do better?

BABA YAGA:

This peaceful mother spectre taunts, haunts,. Her
whispers in yr ear make you grieve and loathe
yrself, harden and sharpen. . Inside you now, there
are many things: bright lily pads, bloated insects.
So it is with everyone. : Thank each tadpole for
joining yr pond , teach yr children to do the same.
And as for the lily pads you honor so--watching yr
pond without fuss will multiply their greenery.

Dear Baba Yaga,

My mother's attempts to break up my marriage, ruin
my closest relationships, and alienate me from my
father have earned her a prolonged estrangement.
Despite my warnings, hints, and unresponsiveness,
she continues to call and spread lies and rumors
about me to our extended family. I do not wish to
forgive, reconcile, or otherwise interact with my
mother. How do I get her to leave me alone?

BABA YAGA:

Yr Mother-Monster's many heads sprout from the
ground. Wherever you go, turnips stink round yr feet
with rotten speech! : But if there is no magic twig
to wither them, work a spell on yr ears (to make
the sounds less grievous) & on yr eyes (to make the
turnips less awful) & on yr heart (which does not
have to eat her words).

HOW DO I HELP MY AGING MOTHER?

Dear Baba Yaga,

How can I help my mother who is losing her mind?
I can't stop feeling sorry for her.

BABA YAGA:

You are not so different from yr mother, and she
doesn't need yr sorry. Sit with her as you are :
dining together in the hot belly of a single beast,
surrounded by mysterious & dangerous goblets,
neither of you more sane nor worthy than the other.
, And, in this way, not alone.

Dear Baba Yaga,

My mom died, and now I feel lost. How can I find
my way?

BABA YAGA:

You were a child picking berries with her mother,
following close behind, when she disappeared into
a secret Grove. , The night came in, you stand with
yr basket alone, even the berries have lost their
meaning. :You will not survive in this wood by
yrself, so go back home on the trail (yr mother's
footprints all over it);wrap yourself with her
blankets. ; Then, reach into the great cold shape
she left behind , as into a hole in a frozen river--
to the other side , to the rush of water, the slick
extraordinary fish. That vast&shocking living can be
yr guide.;

SHOULD I HAVE BEEN A BETTER DAUGHTER?

Dear Baba Yaga,

I lost my dad in my early twenties. We were very close, but as the years pass, I feel guilty for not making more of our time together, for not being a better daughter. What do I do with these regrets?

BABA YAGA:

A daughter is many wooden dolls inside the other, holding an innermost gold tiny doll , the atom of her. ; Born tiny, each year she hops into a new shell for protection. Then the Little One wants out ; cracks herself open to be shining and raw again, irreducible & all-alive!) So if yr father's voice was sometimes muffled through the wooden layers , it is the way of things. Do not hate yrself for growing: Certainly, yr father couldn't: he saw the golden doll in you always (for he first held you at your smallest), & he loved yr layers all the same.

Dear Baba Yaga,

The dying always say that all that matters is love--
the love they've shared with other people. But I am
an introvert, and while I truly love my family and
friends, I prefer to spend most of my time alone or
with my pet. Will I regret not spending more time
with my loved ones, or is there more to life than
other people?

BABA YAGA:

: Humans are just another pumpkin in the patch,
among insect-pumpkins, rat-pumpkins, thought-
pumpkins, god-pumpkins, whale-pumpkins. ; To be
happy you must love somethings (;anythings) with all
yr pumpkin cells, till they glow out. --. & if this
is so, you will not regret yr time in the garden.

Dear Baba Yaga,

After a recent breakup, I've realized how much I use
my partners to create a buffer between me and the
world. On my own now, I feel so stressed all the
time. How do I make my own safety blanket instead
of seeking others to protect me?

BABA YAGA:

Alone, you are raw to the Creatures prowling yr
yard: lions, owls, beasts hooved & clawed.) You
cower inside, even the leaping grasshoppers are
a fright. ; Find a fire -- all need warmth -- and
embroider yr blanket (for you have one already,
be it thin) with the beasts. Over the long nights,
thicken the thread-Creatures into a herd, not
pawing yr skin but covering you, keeping,protecting.
Wear the world you've seen & sewn on yr back, and
be proud.

HOW CAN I KEEP MY PLANTS ALIVE?

Dear Baba Yaga,

How can I keep my plants alive? Nothing seems
to work.

BABA YAGA:

Did you know yr plants are wise gnomes, scheming of
climbing over castle walls to overthrow monarchies
? :Their minds have spires & chambers ,they speak
in many tongues, receiving love notes from the sun
& sending nasty ones to certain detested rabbits.
They are sometimes Lusty, brooding , always
philosophical. . They are Earth, animate. How can
you please them if you ignore their true beings? ;
Listen close , may-be they do not wish to live in yr
house at all.

GOOD IN YR BONES

HOW DO I LEAVE MY MISTAKES BEHIND?

Dear Baba Yaga,

Tiny past mistakes haunt me. Out of nowhere, I'll
think of something stupid I said or did ten years
ago and immediately feel just as cringey as the
moment it happened. I try to learn to let things go,
but they tend to sneak after me anyway and strike
when I least expect it. How do I leave my mistakes
in the past where they belong?

BABA YAGA:

Yr errors are like the little foxes that paw to my
hut; always a fox would be brushing its tail against
my well, or ducking red ears behind a stump. -- So
I said to myself, the Baba: These foxes love you
, why not love them back ! And I began, when I saw
little black eyes in my grasses, to greet the foxes,
slap a fox-rump, even invite a foxie in,tickle its
whiskers, feed it cream. -- Who are you to shoo
away what keeps coming back? Every being in yr woods
is plump with charms & deserves yr friendliness. ;
Treat all the visitors in yr woodshouse kindly, if
you want the woodshouse to be a kindly place..

WHAT IF I'M ACCUSED OF CULTURAL APPROPRIATION?

Dear Baba Yaga,

My friend invited me to a celebration belonging to
their culture, and when I posted a photo of us at
the event, I was accused of cultural appropriation.
I have participated in many similar events over the
years, and I feel I am as respectful as possible.
How do I handle situations like this?

BABA YAGA:

Twelve crows circle a Glass Mountain, each caws a
blessing or a curse. ;Consider each voice,see how
the crows both protect and obscure the Mountain's
beauty. --What does the Mountain mean to you? . What
is it you wish to protect?

Dear Baba Yaga,

I moved to my husband's home state last year to
start a new life and enjoy my husband's community,
but few of his family and friends have given me a
chance. I differ from them in many ways, and I am
too outspoken on things I am passionate about. I try
not to care about others' opinions, but I haven't
made many friends, and it has been lonely. How do I
feel secure enough to stand on my own two legs and
be OK with rejection?

BABA YAGA:

Ponds are always bubbling -- mud shifts, weeds
die, creatures breathe and so the bubbles rise.
, Opinions are like the bubbles: they are of the
pond, but not the pond itself. To love yr own pond's
bubblings too deeply, or to shout at the bubblings
of others, makes little sense. What else lurks in
the pond? . Which fish makes the bubbles rise? Which
plants are silent? ; You are lonely because you
stare at the surface, but the rich dark life squirms
in you, waits.

HOW CAN I STOP WORRYING?

Dear Baba Yaga,

I worry all the time. Sometimes I think I must
be made of worry. These past few years, the focus
of my worry has been my health. I'm constantly
thinking about all that could be wrong with me,
and I often experience psychosomatic symptoms.
How do I become more at home in my body and more
secure in my health?

BABA YAGA:

Worry is: a caterpillar you can watch twisting,
climbing , devouring leaves. . What efforts, what
polka dots! And how sorry in her never-ending
want. ;But you are not the caterpillar--you are the
Watcher, & you can wave to her from the window as
she chews , & go back to yr business.

DO MY C-SECTIONS MAKE ME LESS OF A WOMAN?

Dear Baba Yaga,

I just had a baby, my second. Both were born by
emergency C-section. I feel lucky and happy to have
such a healthy baby, but sometimes I feel like a
half woman or like I didn't earn my babies the way
nature intended. I blame the doctors, the hospital
protocols, and myself for not doing more. How do I
move toward a better sense of self-worth as a woman?

BABA YAGA:

What is a woman, any-way? : Humans are lumps,
made from the same stuff as frogs, rivers, &
leopards. And what is nature? You are the Nature.
--How yr babies arrived is of no consequence, just
as the method of yr own birth does not rival your
hereness. Yr children are yours!. Whoever shames
you sees with a tiny eye. What matters is the three
of you, living.

Dear Baba Yaga,

About a year ago, I survived a terrible health scare
that cost me an ovary. I'm cancer free now, and my
entire life looks different from how it did before
the experience. I feel like I have a second chance,
and I am afraid of wasting it. I don't want cancer
to define my life; how do I move on?

BABA YAGA:

Because you have jumped from one big pond to
another, you feel these are the only two ponds in
the world. But Woods is large, & full of ponds
appearing and disappearing overnight. See: Before
and After does not last for very long, change churns
us on. You wish for a lantern to guide you forever,
but the only lanterns here are fireflies. . Another
fly always beams in when the last one goes. Follow
the wisdoms as they come, don't be scared when they
snuff out.

HOW CAN I LEARN TO LOVE MY AGING BODY?

Dear Baba Yaga,

How can I learn to love my aging body when the whole world tells me that my worth declines with every wrinkle, gray hair, and loose tooth?

BABA YAGA:

In childhood you rode a white horse out of the forest; in youth, a red horse through the market (everyone cheered); now you ride a black horse back into the woods. :No one heralds you. .You are alone with what you always had but barely knew: a strange horse. ;What is the nature of this dark one's mane, trot & mind? , You have nothing left .but the great adventure of the horse.

WHERE DOES MY GENDER IDENTITY COME FROM?

Dear Baba Yaga,

I recently came out as a trans man. Because of
limited resources, for the time being I cannot
pursue surgery or hormones. To validate my maleness,
I've had to explain to many people that masculinity
doesn't originate from male genitalia. But,
privately, I doubt myself. Where *does* my masculinity
come from, and how do I nurture it?

BABA YAGA:

This morning : a snake on my doorstep. Who knows
where the snakely came from? A skull-post in my
fence ; the wood pile ; or my wizard friend's
enchanted lake? And truly the source is not so
easily found, for the snake slithered over all
that land to get here, so was each inch a piece
of source? -- Origins are for dreaming and telling
, & re-telling. But here you are, so manly on my
doorstep, and I admire yr patterns & tongue. :
Feel around and dream up the source if it
strengthens you; but you can always arrive whole
& beam just so .

Dear Baba Yaga,

I had a pregnancy that made me so ill I thought I
would die, and I lost the baby. I wanted a family,
but I can't put my body through that experience
again. Now I can't imagine what the future holds.
Where can I go from here?

BABA YAGA:

You stand before a door blackened by fire.) Turn
from this gutted house,go down the green hill, seek
water -- there is always water, if only a trickle. :
Sit, listen til slowly yr soul shades the color of
grass & creek, and yr body leaches its fear. ; There
is nothing to do but surrender to the sweetness
inside things: this is Healing. When you are well,
yr body will pull you on in fresh strength.

WHY ARE MY FANTASIES SO DARK?

Dear Baba Yaga,

I am a woman with very dark sexual thoughts. The
violations I fantasize about would be unthinkable
to witness or experience in real life, and I judge
myself for being aroused by such imagery. Can you
help me sort it all out?

BABA YAGA:

If you have been hurt , that is another matter.
;But with Lust everything goes topsy-turvy, raggly
& rumply.) Under mortal feets grows a shadow-
world, shifting with monsters,beasts & wonders
--made by gods ,maybe, and the dark tricklings of
human doings, & Mystery . Let it be!:, There is
nothing:wrong with you.

SHOULD I OWN THE WORDS USED AGAINST ME?

Dear Baba Yaga,

When I was a child, other children thought I was
strange and called me a "witch"; in puberty, my
peers called me "slut," "crazy," and "bitch." After
shedding this identity, I have come back around to
what may have sparked those words--and instead of
feeling ashamed, I feel strong and authentic. Should
I trust this feeling, or am I falling into another
identity trap?

BABA YAGA:

Mutter to yrself Language that makes yr bones strong
& yr lungs easy,carry Wyrds that beam&glow in yr
hands : and if such Wyrds were spoken in fear of yr
molten,living core , then how delicious to wield
them as Spells!

AM I A WITCH?

Dear Baba Yaga,

How can I discern which type of witch I am? Or
whether I am indeed a witch at all?

BABA YAGA:

Yr witch-parts are found in bits of raw linen on
trees, scrapings in the hedges. Cows speak when you
are alone. Eating porridge morningly, you crave
to make a thing with sucking roots. ;Approaching
anthills, you invite the ants to tea. : You are
,simply, buried from the waist-down in Earth as yr
arms surge to pull down strings of cosmos.) But do
not mistake witch-parts with a Witch Calling: take
care not to open portals you cannot close::

HOW DO I TELL MY PARENTS THAT I'M A WITCH?

Dear Baba Yaga,

I am a practicing witch who grew up in a
fundamentalist Christian home. For years I have
agonized over whether to share my beliefs with
my parents. It feels my secrets are creating a
rift between us, but I fear their disappointment,
disillusionment, and possibly even disownment.
What would you do?

BABA YAGA:

Each secret is a handful of ashes you throw into a
sack.)The sack is bulging now,an odd thing to keep
in yr house, like a dead animal that chides you from
the corner. It seems you want to throw this sack
into the river! ,but you are afraid of the cost. ;
See: You decide what to do with yr own ashes. ;The
filth that others bring to you--is their doing,
not yrs.

HOW DO I GET MY FAMILY TO ACKNOWLEDGE MY GENDER IDENTITY?

Dear Baba Yaga,

I am a young adult and transgender man. I have told
my family over and over, coming out of the closet
over and over, "I am a man! My name is Xander!"
They simply ignore me. I want them to say my name.
It is as if, by their denial, I am locked in the
closet. They refuse to acknowledge there is a door
to unlock. How can I get respect for my name and
freedom from my family?

BABA YAGA:

Yr family are the ones trapped . in a winter hut.
You wave at the window , they close the shutters.
-- But ,you walk free in the snow, you can follow
any trail & salute any-one else! Yr breath makes
crystals in the cold,spelling X-A-N-D-E-R. :When the
hut-dwellers grow brave, they will open the door &
see yr name shining in the sun .

Dear Baba Yaga,

As a trans woman living under this administration,
I'm faced with society's ugly prejudices against
people like me every day. How do I live in a world
that seemingly hates me without hating it back?

BABA YAGA:

The world is vaster than some humans festering in a
bog, and the forest looks on you with wonder & love,
seeing itself in yr beauty. So follow the love-path
to the raspberry brimming with rain, the goose with
a fiery eye, the bright hill where snakes dance &
good people exalt your brilliance & you are one
hundred thousand suns, illuminating all beings. And
when you hunger, come to my hut. Swap a plate of
yr sorrow for some of my goodly porridge. The world
will bow down to you & eat yr burden whole.

AM I AN IMPOSTOR?

Dear Baba Yaga,

I am a queer person, but I feel uncomfortable in
LGBTQ+ communities and events. I feel like I'm
hogging love, energy, and community that would be
better spent on someone who needs it more. At the
same time, I feel very alone. I know rationally that
queer spaces are for me to enjoy, too! But I can't
shake this feeling that I'm an impostor and I'm
selfishly taking up space that belongs to someone
else. What do I do?

BABA YAGA:

; You tasty little human! Always feeling there is
some badness in you, watching out for it as for a
mean dog loose in the village. But you are all-gold
, look how the flowers gasp at you & you gasp back!
Yr standing in the circle calls others to wake & do
the same. So many others feel your way--would you
tell them they do not belong?

HOW CAN I BECOME A BETTER PERSON?

Dear Baba Yaga,

I have bipolar disorder, and during my worst I've acted in ways that hurt people I care about. I've sought treatment, and I'm horrified by the things I've done. Does having done bad things make me a bad person forever? How can I be good?

BABA YAGA:

My woodshouse does not blame , or punish. When the forest speaks, she says, Shhh. She never says, Put pins in yr skin to know your error – or – You only have so many chances. . See how there is always more of you, in all moments yr lungs are here, & so is the grass? Yr self-knowing is the broth from which you rise, so ladle it on yr limbs & step out. Walk with care : you are learning how to move in this light, but the forest, she believes in yr goodness.

HOW CAN I HEAL FROM AN ABUSIVE PARENT?

Dear Baba Yaga,

My father has been verbally and physically abusive
all my life, which has led me to chronic anxiety,
depression, suicidal thoughts, and eating disorders.
I am lost and dead tired of living with his shadow.
How do I find the bravery to rid myself of him and
find my own way?

BABA YAGA:

Are you running from yr father's shadow, or the one
tied to yr own foot? ; Yr father is a Wretched man,
but I have eaten many men: harder to eat is fear,
shame, hate--these & others which yr father has fed
you all your days., so that yr body casts a scary
shape . Once in safety, hold each of your thrashing
limbs & speak kindly. :For only by smoothing yr own
fur , and brushing yr own fangs, & perfuming yr own
clawed feets, can yr shadow be made welcome.

Dear Baba Yaga,

A month ago I defended myself against a would-
be rapist who attacked me in my own home. I have
received an enormous outpouring of love and support
from friends and family, but my world still feels
like it's on fire. I don't recognize my peaceful,
patient self in the woman who fought back against a
monster, and I feel so quick to anger lately. How do
I find the joy in life again?

BABA YAGA:

Yr new Joy must hold the truth of yr rage for
survival -- you fought for the treasure of life &
yrself, for the Joy waiting on the other side of
that grievous moment. Yr own ferocious Baba-energy
rose then to keep you safe , & now you have a wild
dog to guard the perimeter of yr Joy.;

HOW CAN I HEAL FROM AN ABUSIVE RELATIONSHIP?

Dear Baba Yaga,

After ending an emotionally abusive relationship
with someone I was deeply in love with, I have
cultivated a fulfilling and healthy relationship
with someone else. But I feel haunted by this past
relationship and ashamed for feeling haunted. What
can I do to find peace?

BABA YAGA:

After a night in the branches of a winter tree, you
were brought, half-frozen, to a kind hut,. Of course
you shiver even now. ;You must sit by the fire for a
long time to trust its warmth, to trust that no one
will leave you in the woods again. , This thawing is
not yr error--it is the way of hot.& cold.

HOW DO I FIND PEACE AFTER VIOLENCE ON CAMPUS?

Dear Baba Yaga,

There was recently an incident of sexual and gun violence on our college campus. The school has not responded appropriately, and I'm afraid all the time. How can I ground myself in the middle of such a traumatic time?

BABA YAGA:

, Such harrowing leaves prints in mud and moss, yr path crossed by hooves & paws.   ;You cannot burn the markings, catch or stamp them out. So find a trusted animal and give it a wash. Pouring pail, creek water in the fur, wild eye:. Yr brain needs creature-love, the warmth of hairy pigs and dogs. As you lather their bulk, their feet, sleep gathers & so does rain--the sky will wash away the paw-prints you cannot.

THE FOREST PATH

HOW DO I STOP IDEALIZING NEW SITUATIONS?

Dear Baba Yaga,

When a new event, lover, job, or thing comes into
my life, I paint it gold and hope fervently that
it will be just what I need. When the glitter falls
and reality is revealed in all its flatness, I feel
sad, angry, and less trusting. How do I keep my
imagination but cut the unruly fantasies?

BABA YAGA:

You move as a bird, pecking at one shiny thing after
another,. But the spider is wiser: There is no
thread of a spider's web greater than the rest, and
its treasures--dew & flies--are caught by the whole.
So : be vast! Breathe through yr nose and eyes and
skin, sense the whole of yr intricate being. How
it is held by others, how it cannot be altered or
pleased by any one trinket forever.

HOW DO I FIND MY PASSION?

Dear Baba Yaga,

I'm in my midtwenties, and I have no idea what
I want to do personally or professionally. How
do you find your passion and purpose in a world
that demands all your time and energy to be fed
to the Mundane?

BABA YAGA:

As a child , oncely you woke up with firebird
feathers in yr fist. Gold red and orange, they
glinted wild in yr ordinary hand. You felt the
thrill, but later doubted them ,. Maybe someone
laughed at your talk of the legendary bird, or
you told yrself it wasn't real. So you let the
feathers get dusty under the bed. ; Now, you long
to know there is a firebird somewhere in this
dreary world, that you could hold her by the tail.
-- Crawl under the bed, find those dusty feathers,
see if you can salvage their glint. Recall that bold
silkiness !. Pit-pat closer to the divine beauty
you've known, even if you go afraid & dragging yr
doubts behind you. .

SHOULD I USE MY MOM AS MY MOTIVATION TO SUCCEED?

Dear Baba Yaga,

Like millions of people, my mom lost her home during
the recession. It's my dream to buy her a house
one day, but I make under $16,000 a year and can
barely support myself. Is it wrong for me to want to
take care of my mom, even if I feel like I might go
crazy trying? Is it wrong to use my mom as my main
motivation to succeed in life?

BABA YAGA:

It is not wrong ; to feel the pull of blood, to
take care,. And the house is a little dream on a
lily pad, & in the window glowing candles: money; yr
craving to make greatness from yrself; yr mother's
happiness & yr own. ,But when you swim towards the
lily pad, the pond blackens, the water freezes yr
limbs. See already how you choke & nearly drown. So.
Light the candle in yr hand: This you can give to
yr mother. This you can give to yrself. Is not your
mother alive & well? Maybe one day , she will have
a real house, with real mice, flies, & worries.
Then what? You need a true candle to lead you
through the dark.

SHOULD I CHANGE MY PERSONALITY
TO BENEFIT MY CAREER?

Dear Baba Yaga,

How do I change something that's inherent to my
personality if it's important to my career success?
I've been told I need to be more "detail oriented."

BABA YAGA:

Do yr growing where it matters--in the wild soil,
not any dead fussings about with paper. ;Plant yr
eyes in earth like this: Look at the wormie swaying
on a tree's spit-thread, see the bloody-pawed cat
flick its tail gold, then silver , then gold. Then
watch new eye-bulbs waddle up from the ground. If
they follow you to work, so be it..

HOW DO I STOP JUMPING FROM JOB TO JOB?

Dear Baba Yaga,

I start every new job with so much enthusiasm and
drive, but around the six-month mark I start feeling
restless and go for something else. I don't like
jumping from job to job, and I want to grow in my
current workplace. How do I handle this feeling?

BABA YAGA:

There is an agitated hive in each person ,and the
bees never stop their noise. ; Yr six-months is
like a bee-tree in the forest : if you walk by loud,
shouting & waving yr arms, you will anger the bees &
earn a sting. --But if you creep past & do not make
a sound, the bees will stay inside their murmur. .
and you can go farther on the path. :Remember:: you
do not have to listen to yr apiary.

HOW DO I GIVE A GOOD JOB INTERVIEW?

Dear Baba Yaga,

I've been struggling to figure out my career
path and how to get started. I know my strengths,
but interviews make me so nervous that I can't
articulate my qualities. How do I control my
impostor syndrome and give a good job interview?

BABA YAGA:

You think too much) about yr hands , yr feet, yr
garments, yrself. : Think less about the wild;egg of
You & more about the certain duties. . Work does not
ask you to crack yr soul upon the table & spill out.
-- What does the job demand? Speak of this. ; It is
the others, who are needy , you who stay whole.

Dear Baba Yaga,

Job hunting has been emotionally and financially
draining. After each interview, the employers decide
I'm not a good fit or find a stronger candidate,
and the rejections are starting to affect my self-
esteem. What if I'm not as bright and talented as
I think I am? How can I push on?

BABA YAGA:

No job is so tipsy-wonderful, so dense with cakes -
to earn such sorrow. ; Even when work is yrs,
you must go home & brew the mead and toil the creams
you crave,. Who knows what these Toads are looking
for!). Mind yrself as you would a spiky fairy in
the garden : give her biggish strawberries, build
her the hut of yr dreams. : Then float to the
Toad Buildings, alert & smiling with the luscious
home inside. Come with questions,speak and listen.
Soon , a Toad or two will see yr fitness for
their toadly tasks -- but yr real joy & worthiness
dwells elsewhere.

SHOULD I TAKE ON A CHALLENGING NEW JOB?

Dear Baba Yaga,

I've just been offered a position with a much higher
salary than I currently earn, but I'm afraid of
failing in the new leadership role and the time and
energy it will probably take. Do I stay safe, bored,
and frustrated by my pay? Or do I take a risk, work
harder for more money, and give up some freedom
and flexibility?

BABA YAGA:

Beyond the lake gleams an Emerald castle. To get
there, every-day you must drink all the water!
Yr belly will burst! : Or so you say. But in yr
old pond , you used a stick to catch emerald fish.
Here, you can build a comely boat to glide yr way.
;Is that so deadly-scary? , There are many ways to
cross a Lake.

Dear Baba Yaga,

I worked really hard to get to university, and I love being here. But I'm struggling with the workload. What if I can't manage it? What if my best isn't enough? I'm scared of failing.

BABA YAGA:

Yr eyes are wild apples in this place , they shine at what you see. All you mortals struggle at the beginnings of things, & then recoil,fearing you can't climb to the top of the tree . But you already have the apples that you wished for , the ones crowning the tree. They guide you on; so let them.

Dear Baba Yaga,

I am the boss in a workplace of mostly men, and I
can't help but feel discouraged by the subtle sexism
sometimes. Today one of my employees told me that
all feminists are man-haters and he wishes he'd been
born fifty years ago. My head hurts. Help.

BABA YAGA:

These flailing, angry hedgehogs will soon be slurped
by the wolves of time. Rejoice! Now, tend to your
own soft hedgehog heart; you are not alone in your
hurting, so find those who will keep you safe.
Together, Raise a wail to call the wolves closer.

Dear Baba Yaga,

Every day, I come home from work more irritable than
the day before. My job takes up much of my time,
energy, and goodness, leaving me with little for
myself and others. I feel I have so much to offer in
terms of love and creative works; how do I nurture
myself back each day?

BABA YAGA:

Each morning you put on yr gown of birds, geese &
doves that fly off to do yr bidding.) By Dusk,
you have only a few pigeons to cover yr nakedness
and sing to you. , But these are sun-birds ;
stranger beasts creep at night. Invite the cats and
lurking owls to be yr nightly garments, let them
perch on yr head to make a crown, let the snakes
wind round yr arms as living jewels. You can be a
new creature once the day is done:: yr self-shadows
playing with the moon's shadows, crafting who knows
what goodliness.

HOW CAN I GO FOR MY GOALS WHILE LIVING
WITH A CHRONIC SICKNESS?

Dear Baba Yaga,

I'm sick. I have been for a long time, and I will be indefinitely. I want to do something extraordinary with my life . . . art and writing. But I feel like all of my energy gets used up by everyday drudgery, and I spend the rest of my time in bed. How can I prioritize art?

BABA YAGA:

Watching the greenest frog leap, the pale toad feels weaker. But even frogs are sick sometimes & dying always, and every life is drudgery if it is not loved. .Can you know & adore yr life, small and lurching as it may seem? There is a well in you , juicy. Find the moment, hour, when you are freshest, & the well will brim and multiply with tadpoles. Dwell & drink until the well dries up. Then, watered so, hop on as you can.

HOW DO I STAY ROOTED IN A TRANSIENT LIFE?

Dear Baba Yaga,

My profession requires me to move often, and while
I enjoy the rich variety of experiences and the
relationships I've developed in each place, I often
feel dislocated, fragmented. How can I preserve
the best elements of my transient life while
establishing and nurturing deep roots?

BABA YAGA:

: Trees cannot travel & Beasts cannot root, so
you must become something in between: a Traveling
Gardener of Many Trees. , After rooting a tree in
each place;come back oftenly to water the tree,
sing yr best songs to its sap, bury sweetmeats in
the soil -- and if you must be away for long, send
messages & delicacies on a crow.) Over years, you
will be the Keeper of a secret, far-flung forest ,
though you look like a rover in the desert.

HOW DO I DEAL WITH HOMESICKNESS?

Dear Baba Yaga,

My family and I moved to America from Russia. I hate it here. How do I go back? I am only twelve!

BABA YAGA:

Oh child, you;are a small Creature on a leaf, carried to a strange new pond. You long for the pond you knew--such is the painful,mortal way. ;One day you may go back, but for now , look and see: the tree hiding a witch, the ladybug landing near, the young duck paddling beside, as lost&itchy as you--& all these you may befriend. , And, when you are itchiest and saddest, close yr eyes & say:

This leaf knows where to go
This water is wise
This forest knows my name.

SHOULD I LEAVE THE CITY I HATE
IF IT MEANS LEAVING MY PARTNER?

Dear Baba Yaga,

For so long I've wanted to move out of the city
I live in, but I haven't done so because my partner
wouldn't be able to come with me. I love him dearly,
but I hate living here. How do I deal with this
restlessness and frustration? Should I stay or
move away?

BABA YAGA:

You live in a cramped,house, trees stumpy, village
ugly,. :Open yr oven door & the windows, unbuckle
your belt, unknot your ropes, unbraid your hair::and
all at once it comes, the spring river breaking out
from its dirty ice. Get in, carried so fast, and
louder than all yr fears, say - I AM THE RIVER ,
THERE IS NO STOPPING - and watch yrself go out, out
the village gate!

HOW CAN I HAVE A WHOLESOME PREGNANCY UNDER CAPITALISM?

Dear Baba Yaga,

I'm newly pregnant, and all I want to do is walk slowly under trees and lie down on moss. I'm angry that capitalism prevents me from simply breathing and growing my baby. I want to throw all my electronics away and disappear into the forest, but I'm a caretaker by profession and feel stuck. What can I do?

BABA YAGA:

Every beast responds to salt in the eyes, even the grinding beast you speak of. Once a day, throw salt into the clocks & sprint for the hairy hills. Yr sweat will make a pool under your body, on top of which you can float with yr big belly , moss growing between yr toes. -- Don't let the beast take all from you, even if you can't salvage everything you need from its maw.)

Dear Baba Yaga,

When I was a child, before I had even heard my
ancestors' tales about you, you would come to me in
dreams. You still visit me, handing me brooms and
telling me to work, and you're the one who nudged
me to visit Russia and learn to work with plants. I
long for the folklore and stories of my people, but
my grandparents are gone, and my parents keep quiet.
How can I keep our traditions alive when I see the
fire of my ancestry slowly dying?

BABA YAGA:

So early you conjured me -- the tales live deep
in yr mind-forest, without anyone saying. ; Yr
family gate may be closed, but there are other ways
into the village. : Seek out those who share yr
longing, kneel with them at the fire.) And look
to the plants of the old land, the bones and books
yr people left: all will wake something. , Most of
all, know this: You are the living story: the tales
loop&dive in your blood like fish. You are the ,
best kindling for the fire, so Speak out loud to
yrself , and you will hear the many things you know
but have not yet discovered.

HOW DO I DEAL WITH CLIMATE CHANGE?

Dear Baba Yaga,

I carry the painful knowledge that our world is
changing and dying. I cannot protect my young
children from the future, and I am afraid to infect
my loved ones with my anxiety. How can we have
inner peace while confronting the rising tide of
environmental collapse?

BABA YAGA:

I have watched Earth turn over many times, green
& red & black & gold: no species, world-state, or
life-web stays. ; You worry that nothing of yrs
will live past the Changing, but witness yrself in
the bee & the water, in the becoming & vanishment
of both, in what comes next -- and you will know
better. The Changing brings fear & sorrow, but
Wonder lurks in the same field, gathers the two
sobbing children in her arms, and holds. Wonder,
she is the only one who stays; anyone can join
her,walking into each new Earth. : And in the
meantimes, care for what is here -- but don't
ask for what is foolish, for the Here to be the
same forever.

ARE WE HEADING FOR A CULTURE WAR?

Dear Baba Yaga,

I fear we are headed for a culture war. Fear of
scarcity feeds fear of "the other" and leads to
violence. How do I stay true to my values without
falling way to fundamentalism and rigidity?

BABA YAGA:

Fears pop up like rabid cabbages : no scythe so
quick to lop them off. , Still, scything pleases
my slick liver -- pleased to watch the heads roll,
pleased to see Rabbits sniff the leaves. , The
cabbages slow near my pine-tree friends, who bend to
look. ;They regard the cabbages without tensing ,
though they know fear's poison. Winter & wind heavy
on their shoulders these long years, but they do
not break. Their needles soft as rabbits , alert as
snow. My scythe glints,night is coming. Another year
in the woods.::

Dear Baba Yaga,

My brother voted for Donald Trump and feels no
shame or regret. I love my brother, and we used to
be very close, but I don't know quite how to have
a relationship with him anymore. I am a lawyer who
works on behalf of women and immigrants, and I don't
know what to say to someone who betrayed everything
I fight for. I will always love my brother, but what
if I'm frightened of the person he is growing up
to be?

BABA YAGA:

There are many ugly things in my forest, many
sicknesses that eat the leaves of trees I love,
grubs that hatch in the fur of gorgeous animals.
For as long--as I have lived & watched these woods,
there have been ill creatures, staggering. ,Then
there is a fire, or a great death, & there are
nutrients for a fresher life. Yr world is due for a
fire. ;and yr sorrow & fear is that of someone who
loves a sick thing, whose kind will not survive.
This is worth grieving.)But the fire will come.

Dear Baba Yaga,

In a world that seems evermore focused on placing
power in systems that harm nature, racialized and
marginalized people, and the powerless--where is
my energy best placed?

BABA YAGA:

Place it in the cauldron nearest & already
attended by Witches--for why make yr own cauldron
or worry to choose, when so many cauldrons boil with
ancient rage & love & the calling to remedy harm.
Stir the pot well ; add the goodly spices & the
unexpected juice; wring in yr sweat , yr swollen
heart, yr fellowship , the tears of perfect animals.
Then drink a ladle-full,stir again , & feed it to
the Others.

Dear Baba Yaga,

I feel weak in the soul and full of rage at the
state of the world. How would you encourage warriors
to refuel? How can we bring the Baba Yaga energy
into our lives and live out our wisdom?

BABA YAGA:

Earth--wild, foaming species & gobbling, hungry,
yelling into lava, wrapping itself in clouds,
heaving, contracting--was not made to please you. ;
Wishing for Earth to be otherwise, you are small &
angry as a bee. Baba energy is chaos energy. Baba is
carried on the hot black river of doom, because Baba
is the doom & the quiet on the other side. Relax
into Chaos. Be the river that dooms you., when it
spits you out, you will know how to act in wisdom.

HOW DO I FIND MY ROLE IN THE REVOLUTION?

Dear Baba Yaga,

How do I find my role in the revolution?

BABA YAGA:

Pull yr Intellect from yr body like the spine from
a fish ; Plunge her into the inky pond of Desire &
Mystery --fish her out, dark & dripping, strangely
nourished , wiser than you,scarier, richer in
direction, -- send this stickly daemon out into the
streets ahead, follow behind like a moon, cheering.:

HOW CAN I SURVIVE THE APOCALYPSE?

Dear Baba Yaga,

We are living in an actual global disaster, and
the world feels doomed. What will happen to us? What
can I do when I am afraid for the safety and well-
being of myself, my loved ones, and everyone else on
the planet?

BABA YAGA:

What happens now , has always been: all teeming
things in survival , new forms arising, some deadly
to others. And Humans, as always, falling through
holes they made or never mended. ;But Earth is not
failing. Earth is pushing out flower-heads & cells.
There is enough rock to absorb yr fear & release
it like heat. Do what I do: Each morning I wash my
feets, make tea , crack eggs, visit my bee-friends.,
forage leeks & spicy radishes. I read Plants &
listen for wolves. Gather yrself into a big bundle
, even as yr legs kick out the sides like a bloody
foal's & fear slithers from the cloth .. Let the
bundle be the baby you sing to & feed. Then gather
the others, mend the gaps.)

HOW CAN I FEEL WHOLE?

Dear Baba Yaga,

I sometimes feel an emptiness in my life, like I
don't have a purpose or what I'm doing isn't notable
enough. I am still young, but this feeling haunts
me. What can I do to feel more whole?

BABA YAGA:

All yr days feel like carrying water in a sieve ; yr
hands splashed with Drain. But if you are made of
many tiny holes, the openings go both ways: The world
fills you even now. For is the Earth not whole,
though troubled? And are you not a part of it , a
sieve washed with its meaning?:

ACKNOWLEDGMENTS

I am grateful to playwright Eva Suter, who, after
my surprising encounter with Baba Yaga, suggested
that an advice column in the witch's voice might
be worthwhile. To Jia Tolentino, my editor at the
Hairpin, for running the original column on the
beloved website. Thank you to agent Adriann Ranta
Zurhellen and Andrews McMeel editor Allison Adler,
for believing in this book. To artist Katy Horan,
for making my illustration dreams come true. Thank
you to the Tasajillo Residency, for keeping me
in fine foods, wine, and lodging while I wrote a
good chunk of these pieces. To Fernando, for being
a first reader and making sure Baba didn't say
anything too crazy.

Most of all, thank you to everyone who wrote in
with a question for Baba Yaga. It takes bravery to
lay your most intimate problems at anyone's feet,
especially at the calloused old claws of Baba Yaga.
Without your vulnerability and trust, this book
would not have been possible.

Enjoy *Poetic Remedies for Troubled Times from Ask Baba Yaga* as an audiobook, wherever audiobooks are sold.